WALT DISNEY's

Sleeping Beauty

SO-AGV-887

© Disney. Published by **Egmont Imagination (India) Ltd.,**
Dani Wooltex Compound, 158, Vidyanagari Marg, Kalina, Santacruz (E),
Mumbai - 400 098, India, under license from WD Consumer Products,
a division of WD India Pvt. Ltd. All rights reserved.

Once upon a time there lived a King and Queen who longed so much to have a baby. And when they finally had a daughter they were very happy.

They called her Aurora, which means dawn – like the sun at dawn she brightened their lives.

People from far and near flocked to the castle to convey their good wishes. The three good fairies Flora, Fauna and Merryweather also arrived to bless Aurora. Flora blessed the princess with beauty while Fauna blessed her with the gift of song.

But as Merryweather was about to give her gift to the baby, a gust of wind blew open the doors.

There was a flash of lightning and a flash of thunder. Suddenly a bright flame began to burn in the hall, which took the shape of a woman. The wicked fairy Maleficent had arrived and to show anger at not having been invited she cursed the baby...

"On her sixteenth birthday your daughter shall prick her finger on the spindle of a spinning wheel and die!" she said. The good fairies could not undo the curse, but they changed it. "She shall not die, but sleep until a kiss of true love breaks the spell," said Merryweather.

The King and Queen would do anything to protect their daughter.

The King ordered that all spinning wheels in the Kingdom be burned. But the fairies thought this was not safe enough.

"We will raise your daughter and bring her back when the curse ends on her sixteenth birthday," they offered.

So they brought the baby to the woods and as the years went by she grew more and more beautiful.

On her sixteenth birthday, the good fairies sent Aurora out into the woods to pick berries, so that they had time to prepare a party. She walked along happily singing when suddenly she heard someone say: "What a lovely voice!"

Aurora turned around and saw the most wonderful young man and without thinking she invited him to the cottage that very night.

❧ ❦ ❧

When Aurora came back to the fairies she was all excited. "I think I have fallen in love," she said and told them all about the young man in the wood and the invitation. The fairies knew the time had come to tell the truth.

They told Aurora the whole story
and then they all began the long
journey back to the castle.

But all Aurora could think of was
the young man who would come to
the cottage in vain.

When Princess Aurora arrived at the castle, Maleficent put a spell on her and in a trance she went to a secret room in a tower where Maleficent had hidden a spinning wheel. Aurora touched the spindle and fell into a deep sleep.

In the meantime, Flora had found out that Aurora's young man was Prince Phillip. Now it was time to find him - only his kiss could save the Princess.

That night when Prince Phillip went to visit Aurora in the cottage he was surprised by the terrible Maleficent. "Capture him!" she shouted to her henchmen, "he is the only one who has the power to break my curse on Aurora."

Prince Phillip was brought to
Maleficent's dungeon and there she
revealed to him that his girl from
the wood was really
a Princess.

Luckily the good fairies found Maleficent's dungeon and with wisdom and magic they managed to save the Prince from Maleficent and her henchmen.

"These weapons will help you triumph over all evil," they said and gave him a Shield of Virtue and a Sword of Truth.

Then Prince Phillip rushed off to save his Princess.

As he got close to the palace, Maleficent let a wall of thorns grow up in front of him, but he cut his way through that. Then she turned herself into a fuming dragon.

It seemed an impossible battle, but after an exhausting fight with the weapons the good fairies had given him, Prince Phillip finally won and raced through the palace gates.

In a room in the tower he found his beautiful, sleeping Aurora.

"Wake up, my lovely Princess," he whispered and kissed her gently on her lips.

Aurora woke up and smiled to her prince. Together they left the chamber and descended the stairs. The Prince brought her to her parents and they were happily reunited.

And that night everyone at the castle celebrated. Princess Aurora and Prince Phillip danced in each other's arms the whole night.

"Who would have dreamed that all this would end so happily," the king sighed and felt very pleased.